# OSCAR
## THE ORGO

For Olivia, Ian and Lewis - RJF

For Eleanor and Iris - FF

**ORGO PRESS**
First published in 2020 by Orgo Press

Text copyright © R.J. Furness 2020
Illustrations copyright © Fiona Fletcher 2020

Written By
**R.J. Furness**

Illustrated By
**Fiona Fletcher**

# HAVE YOU EVER HEARD OF AN ORGO?

Have you ever heard of an orgo?
They're a creature you might not know.
With long, thin necks, and only two legs,
they tend to hang out in the snow.

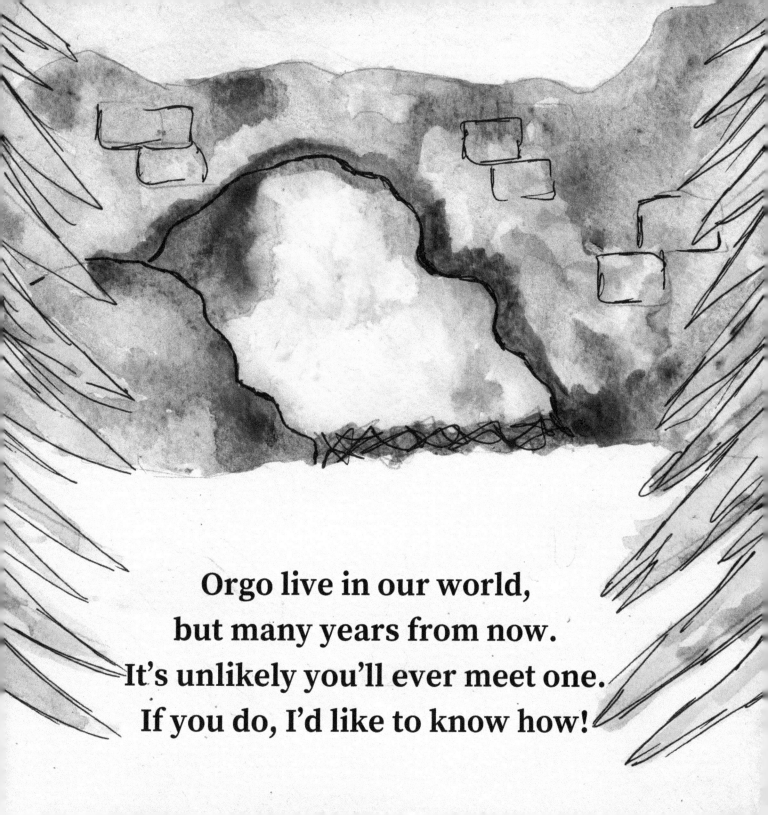

Orgo live in our world,
but many years from now.
It's unlikely you'll ever meet one.
If you do, I'd like to know how!

Our story starts with an orgo,
Oscar was his name.
When he hatched from his egg one winter,
he was born with a big fluffy mane.

Apart from the fur on his shoulders,
Oscar was a lumpy pink thing.
But there was something special about Oscar,
because Oscar loved to sing.

All through the day, and all through the night,
Oscar just wouldn't stop.
His mother would beg him to take a break,
but Oscar would start from the top.

From Oscar's cave, you could always hear
the sound of a cheerful tune.
'Enough is enough,' his mother cried.
But Oscar would not give up soon.

'It's time to eat,' said
Oscar's mum.
'You need to take a rest.'

'Never,' said Oscar,
carrying on.
'I'm singing 'cause singing
is best.'

The orgo mother was in despair.
She'd never heard such a sound.
Oscar's singing was far too noisy,
and a crowd had gathered around.

Many more orgo had come to the cave,
to see what the fuss was about.
But they didn't expect, until they arrived,
that Oscar could sing without doubt.

'Orchids!' Mum shouted.
'It's time for tea.'
But Oscar went on with
his song.
'You'll have to eat soon,'
his mum tried again.
'You'll starve if you go on
too long.'

'I have to sing,'
was Oscar's reply.

'I don't know why
I can't stop!'

Then he sang some more while his mother tucked in,
and ate up her orchid crop.

As day turned to night, all the orgo left,
leaving Oscar and Mum alone.
And still Oscar sang from his dark, cosy cave...
but now he had changed his tone.

'Your tune is different,' said Oscar's mum.
'Why do you sound so strange?'
'I really don't know,' Oscar replied.
'My voice just decided to change.'

Oscar's mum was becoming sad,
and they both just needed some sleep.
But still Oscar sang, and sang some more,
and Mum began to weep.

Suddenly, another noise could be heard,
but this one sounded quite scary!

It wasn't coming from Oscar,
and Mum was feeling wary.

'Gliders!  Oh no!' yelled Oscar's mum,
who appeared to be quite upset.

'We need to run.  We need to hide.
Gliders are too big a threat.'

'Those beasts smell bad, and they'll steal our food,'
Mum was going wild.
'It's okay, Mum, I know what to do,'
replied her orgo child.

Stumbling around on his wobbly legs,
Oscar moved in the wrong direction.
'No. Oscar, no.  You're going the wrong way.
We need to hide in this section.'

Oscar breathed in, then sang
really loud,
as he headed towards the gliders.
'It's okay, Mum. Really it is.
I can scare off the outsiders.'

When the gliders swooped inside the cave,
Oscar stood brave and bold.
He sang, and he sang, and he sang even more,
while he shivered in the cold.

The gliders beat their wings in fright,
and tumbled around in the air.
But Oscar didn't seem worried.
He didn't appear to care.

Mum moved forward and started to sing,
joining in with her son.
It seemed the gliders weren't fans of their songs,
but Oscar was having fun.

In no time at all the gliders flew off,
leaving the cave in a hurry.

'Oscar,' said Mum, 'now we know why you sing!
When you sing, we don't need to worry!'

'The gliders won't come and steal our food,
as long as we sing our song.'
'Yes, Mum,' grinned Oscar. 'But what is a glider?
I haven't been here very long.'

'Tomorrow,' said Mum.
'I'll explain it all.
For now, we need some rest.'
But Oscar didn't answer...

**He'd fallen asleep in their nest.**

# About The Author

R. J. Furness has been passionate about great stories since he was able to read. At an early age, he would frequently create new characters, worlds and creatures, then write crazy tales all about them. However, until now, he has always kept those ideas completely secret. After having a lifelong interest in animals, music and anything spawned from pure imagination, R.J.'s first love is now his wife and children. Over time, he has also developed an overwhelming desire for mugs of tea and good biscuits to dunk. He lives in Southport, England, with his family, a dog and several fish, chickens and quails.

Find out more about R.J. Furness and his extraordinary worlds…

www.rjfurness.com

or please come and say hello on social media…

Twitter: @rjfurness
Facebook: furnesswrites

# About The Illustrator

Fiona has been a keen artist since the days of drawing on her parent's walls as a toddler. Through school, she always pursued the artistic and creative classes which allowed her to find her own flare. In 2017, after having two children, Fiona began her artistic business, Menagerie Of Mayhem, painting in bright rainbow colours and finding her place in the art world. All this, whilst also being able to spend all the time in the world with her daughters, going on school trips, days out at the zoo and more!

Explore more of Fiona's work on Etsy, and get your exclusive Oscar merchandise…
menagerieofmayhem.etsy.com

Find Fiona on Facebook - www.facebook.com/menagerieofmayhem
Follow Fiona on Instagram - www.instagram.com/menagerie_of_mayhem

# For More Orgo Adventures, Try The Orgo Runners Series!

## Suitable For Readers Aged 6 And Over

Printed in Australia
AUHW012024240420
326618AU00028B/498

9 781916 163799